BEGINNER READER

RAINBOW magic™

The Fairy Treasure Hunt

Cardiff Libraries
www.cardiff.gov.uk/libraries

Llyfrgelloedd Caerdydd
www.caerdydd.gov.uk/llyfrgelloedd

Orchard Beginner Readers are specially created to develop literacy skills, confidence and a love of reading.

ORCHARD BOOKS
Carmelite House, 50 Victoria Embankment. EC4Y 0DZ
Orchard Books Australia
Level 17/207 Kent Street, Sydney, NSW 2000
A Paperback Original

First published in the USA in 2010 by Scholastic Inc
This edition published in 2016 by Orchard Books

HiT entertainment

A CIP catalogue record for this book is available from the British Library.

ISBN 978 1 40833 966 4

1 3 5 7 9 10 8 6 4 2

Printed in China

MIX
Paper from
responsible sources
FSC® C104740
FSC
www.fsc.org

Orchard Books is an imprint of Hachette Children's Group and published by The Watts Publishing Group Limited,
an Hachette UK company.

www.hachette.co.uk

BEGINNER READER

RAINBOW magic™

The Fairy Treasure Hunt

Daisy Meadows

ORCHARD

The morning sun shines on Fairyland.
The Jewel Fairies are excited.
"I can't believe today is the day!" says India.

"Our Fairy Test is finally here," Sophie agrees. "We've been training for so long."

Sophie looks around the cottage at her sisters.
They are all fairies in training.
Once they pass their Fairy Test, they
will be full fairies.

"I wonder what our challenge will be,"
Sophie says.
"There's only one way to find out,"
says Emily.

After breakfast, the fairies fly
to the royal meadow.

As soon as they arrive, sparkles swirl in the sky.
Queen Titania lands in front of them.

"Welcome to your Fairy Test," the queen says.
"Your challenge will be a treasure hunt!"

"I will hide each of your jewels somewhere in Fairyland," the queen explains.
She twirls her wand, and the seven gems magically appear.

"Believe in yourselves and help each other find the jewels," she says.
Then the colourful gems disappear right before the fairies' eyes.

"Find your seven jewels and you will pass the test," the queen smiles at the young fairies. "Soon we'll be full fairies!" Sophie whispers to the others.

"Remember, the magic is inside you," the
queen says. "Good luck, Jewel Fairies!"
The wise fairy twirls her wand and disappears.

"Where should we start?" Emily asks.
"She didn't give us any clues," Scarlett adds.

"Yes, she did," says India. "She said the magic is inside us."
"Maybe our magic will help us find our jewels," says Emily.
"But how?" asks Sophie.

"Just trust your magic," says India. "Come on!"

India grabs Sophie's hand, and all the Jewel Fairies fly into the air.

Their wings sparkle in the sunlight.

"I see something!" Chloe yells with delight.
"There are golden sparkles in that tree."
Chloe dives over for a closer look.
"My jewel is hiding in a bird's nest," she says.

The fairies split up to search for the other
magical gems.
India follows a trail of pale pink sparkles into
the castle.
"My moonstone is under the queen's
pillow!" she says with a giggle.

Amy and Scarlett see some sparkles in the royal garden.
Scarlett's red jewel is in the strawberry patch.
Amy finds her purple jewel in a lilac bush.

Sophie searches the palace grounds,
but she does not see blue sparkles anywhere.

"Look how the fountain glitters," Lucy says.
"It must be fairy magic."

Lucy zips down and plucks her jewel from the top of the fountain.
"Hooray!" she exclaims.

The fairies fly to the Fairyland Forest.
Sophie and Emily are still looking for
their gems.

Emily spies a swirl of green sparkles coming
from a hole in an old log.
She peeks inside.

"Well, hello there!" Emily says to a family of rabbits. "Thank you for keeping my jewel safe."
Emily gives each rabbit a pat. Then she takes her green gem.

"We only have to find one more jewel," Chloe
says.
The fairies turn to Sophie.
"I haven't seen blue sparkles anywhere,"
Sophie says sadly. "Maybe I don't have any
magic inside me."

"You just need to believe in yourself," says Amy.

"What's your favourite part of being a fairy?" Scarlett asks.

Sophie thinks for a moment. "I love to make wishes come true," she says.

"Maybe you need to make your own wish now," Emily suggests.

Sophie takes a deep breath. "I'll try. Will you help me?" she asks.

The fairies nod and form a circle.

Sophie recites her wish. It sounds like a song.

"Magic might, magic may,
Be with us this very day.
In a circle fairies bow,
May magic grant my wish right now."

The fairies touch their wands together.
A burst of blue sparkles appears.

"Look, the sparkles make a path," India says.
The Jewel Fairies follow the trail.

"The sparkles lead through here," says Sophie
as she pushes back some leafy branches.
She gasps with surprise.

Queen Titania is standing in the clearing,
and she has Sophie's blue jewel in her hands!

"Congratulations on finishing the treasure hunt!" the queen exclaims. "You found all the jewels. This calls for a celebration!"

Now the fairies in training are full fairies.
The queen gives them necklaces.
Hanging from each necklace is the special
jewel each fairy found.

"This has been a magical day," says India.
"Yes," Sophie agrees. "It's been a wish
come true!"